Trittany

*A fiction-reality tale of
'The Next Step'*

Brittany

Trevor takes my hand as we near the studio where we film The Next Step. I'm wearing a designer blue jean dress with gold buttons. Today is the first day of filming for season 4. It has been five months since the premier of Season 3 and the fans are getting feisty for more episodes. It was unbelievable how through the show we had found real love, it's all such an amazing coincidence that we date on the show as well as in real life. It was a miracle I came to auditions that day otherwise

I wouldn't of been able to build this romantic relationship with Trevor. Trevor stops at the stage door, and turns round cupping my face in his hands, he then slowly leans in and kisses me. His kisses are so real and whenever we kiss it feels like there's a lightning bolt going through our bodies. I never want the kiss to end, but of course it does because we can't be late for filming!

I've grown up a lot since season 1, when I wore spotty and stripy clothes and a childish hairstyle, I now have shoulder length hair, dyed a smoky brownish blonde. Trevor twirls a loose strand of my hair and slides it behind my ear. I give him a peck on the lips, then we rejoin hands and walk through stage A door.

Trevor

*Waiting in the studio is all my
plans, the candles, and all of
the cast in the positions I
assigned them. As soon as we
walk through the door everyone
starts dancing my choreography
to 'Coming home'.*

*Brittany gasps, wondering
what on earth is going on! I
silently laugh to myself as I see
her stunned, shocked face.
Lamar Flips back landing just
behind Victoria and lifts her up
into a helicopter lift. Samantha
jumps into Eldon's arms and
twists round him, while Myles*

grabs Briar and pulls her into a complicated double spin, and all the others do their part. The dance goes on and as the music has its last upbeat note I pull Brittany in and we dance together. When it's done I grab Brittany's hand and pull her into the middle of the floor where candles form a love heart around us. I hold her hand for a minute as she gives me a confused look, I fiddle with the pretty diamond engagement ring in my pocket, this is it!

Brittany

I wait for Trevor to do something, wondering what the heck is happening?! Trevor eventually slowly gets down on one knee and I gasp, holding my hand to my mouth, I can't believe what's happening! He soon pulls out a perfect little silver ring and holds my hand in his, still. "Brittany Lynn Raymond, these last 10 months have been the best of my entire life! You have turned my world around for the better. You're the key to my heart and I wouldn't want you any other way, you're my one and only. If I had never met you, I would grow old on my own and be a miserable old man for eternity." I was oblivious to everyone laughing at this statement, this moment was for just me and Trevor. He pauses for a minute, obviously nervous but keeping his confidence at the same time. "So that is why,....." He continues "I ask you to make me the most loved and happiest man alive by becoming Mrs. Tordjman!" He finishes and nervously glances up at me waiting for my answer....It must have felt like an eternity to him but it only took a moment for it all to sink in, that if I said yes I would be an engaged, almost MARRIED WOMAN!

"Maybe,.....I'm just kidding, of course I'll marry you!" I scream and he slides the beautiful ring onto my left hand ring finger gently, then gets up and scoops me up in his strong safe arms, kissing me passionately. "I love you" I whisper to him, "I love you just as much, times a billion!" he whispers back. Everyone's jumping up and down with excitement and I'm feeling stunned, nervous, excited and happy, plus

surprised, extremely — after all,
we are only 20 years old!

Trevor

I hug Brittany intimately, then my bro's Lamar and Isaac pull us apart and remind me a million times that I'm getting married, but I don't need reminding! I do some flips with them, but my eyes are on Brittany as she talks to Victoria and Alexandra as Jordan and Taveeta hug her. I grin at her happily as she smiles kindly at me, this must be love!

Later that night.....

At around 10pm I'm sitting with my arm firmly around Brittany in our fancy modern glass apartment home, as we watch the film 'Crazy, stupid, love', her favourite and eat banana chips. I drink a beer as Brittany sips down red wine. Then we kiss each other goodnight and go to our rooms. I think about how in just 4 months time we will be MARRIED! I lie in bed with my plain dark blue duvet around me. I think about Brittany in just the room next to me, I text her saying 'goodnight and I love you times a billion more than you love me!' We may live together but texting is romantic somehow. As I'm thinking about this I hear a bleep and turn to my phone where a text has appeared from Brittany saying 'how is that possible when I love you a billion times infinity and beyond?!' I answer saying 'The magic of love makes that possible' then I switch off my phone and fall into a deep dreamy sleep.

Brittany

When I wake up the next day I go downstairs to find Trevor has prepared a romantic breakfast in the kitchen, with a fresh red rose in a vase on the centre of the table. I peer around the kitchen and wonder where he could be! Suddenly I feel two strong hands and arms wrap around my waist from behind, and pull me in close so I can feel his breath on my neck. I turn my head and look up at Trevor's handsome face and pull him in for a kiss. We kiss for a while then I say "thank you for breakfast, it looks delicious!"

"Just like you!" he says romantically. Then we sit down and eat the fluffy waffles with bananas and syrup, not very healthy for 2 dancers but it's an occasional treat! I was glad we had a day off on Saturday, because that meant I had Trevor to myself all day. Once we've finished breakfast, Trevor and I pop upstairs to shower. I let the warm drizzles of water cover my bare back and wash my face. When I've finished my shower I slip on my dressing gown and put some lip gloss, concealer, blush, mascara, eyebrow pencil and eye liner on, my usual, then tie my short straight hair into a pony tail. I do this In front of my dressing table. Then brush my hair and teeth. Afterwards I pull a white floaty top on and black and white rose patterned shorts with a beautiful blue gem stone necklace around my neck that Trevor gave me along with my delicate engagement ring. Then I take out my pony-tail and go back down the glass spiral staircase to the kitchen. Trevor is sitting in one of the dark plush wooden seats, flipping

through wedding magazines,
which surprises me! "Are you
sure you can plan the
honeymoon, ALL on your own?!"
I ask, a little bit worried,
"Calm down babe, I can handle
it! TRUST ME, we'll be married
in 4 months, that's something
you'll have to learn to do!" he
says calmly,
"I do trust you, I'm sorry, it's
just I've never done this
before!" I say apologetically,
"I know, it's ok. I haven't
either." Trevor says soothingly.
I sit on his knee and stroke his
grey muscle top. Then he gently
pulls me in for a long kiss!

Trevor

3 months and 3 weeks later
(9th July)

Finally Season 4 of the Next
Step is finished and the premier
was 1 week ago!
In just one week's time I'm
going to be a happily married
man, but before then Brittany
and I have our bachelor and
bachelorette parties. It will be
hard staying apart from her for
a whole entire week but I know
my groomsmen Isaac, Lamar and
my big Bro will keep me busy
and entertained.

Brittany

Leaving Trevor will be so hard, I have packed my bags to go and stay at Jordan's with my bridesmaids Jordan, Victoria, Alexandra and the maid of honour, my sister, Samantha. I will be partying hard all week, during my last days of being a un-married woman.

I kiss Trevor goodbye as I step into Vic's pure white dazzling new Porsche. When I arrive at Jordan's we all do childishly fun things like roasting marshmallows over the barbecue and doing prank phone calls! It's so fun but so naughty! I miss these kind of days, so I'm glad I get to do it once more before I'm a mature (not completely) married woman. At 4am we all fall to sleep in Jordan's old tent, which we set up in the back yard!

The next night.....

When we get to 8pm the next night, we decide to go for a more adult approach to my ongoing bachelorette party, all the girls drink some beer and wine, and we let Vic have a glass of wine naughtily, she's 17. Then we go to sleep under the stars on Jordan's old trampoline with blankets over us!

Trevor

"I imagine the girls will be
sleeping by now!" says Isaac,
"Yeah, girls are boring, why you
doing this bro?" asks Lamar,
"Excuse me, are you talking
about my fiancé?" I joke!
We all glug down some beer
then order pepperoni and
pepper pizza with extra hot
sauce on. We easily eat it all
and my brother says we should
watch 'The Avengers'. We do, I
realise I won't be watching
anything like this with Brittany,
but hey, she's worth it! We play
truth or dare and I end up

getting dared to jump of the really high diving board into Isaacs pool! It's a fun night!

Brittany

5 days later
(15th July)

As I wake up on Sunday morning, I realise today is my wedding day, when I'll see Trevor again and be wed to him to be with him for ever! As I walk downstairs all my gals are sitting there: Victoria, Alexandra, Jordan and Samantha, my loving sister, who is already married. They are all so supportive, I smile at them as they chorus "Go girl, you're getting married!". An hour later

Taveeta arrives with my dress. Taveeta is my bridesmaid too but she couldn't make it to the bachelorette party because her boyfriend had a holiday with her. All the girls do my makeup and my hair and Samantha helps me into my dress. When they're done I look into my long silver and polished glass mirror at myself. I have a pretty ombré brown and blonde curled short hairstyle and a pure silver and diamonds tiara, like a real princess, with a long long white veil, I have white eyeshadow, 'Cleopatra' black eyeliner, dark pink lip-gloss and pink blush. I wear my diamond necklace with diamond earrings. My dress··· my dress... my dre...... It's stunningly gorgeous. It's a beige— white sleeveless dress that's slim at the waist but then pops out at the skirt area and the neck at the top has gems and white dainty flowers spread about, with a white silk belt at the waist. I look at my pearly white strap pump heels. I glance down at my white and blue diamond engagement ring. The bridesmaids are all wearing knee length sky blue silk dresses. Looking gorgeous! Finally my own fairytale!

Trevor

*I smile at all my groomsmen
looking handsome in their
Tuxedos and then I see myself
in my suit with a blue tie and I
know today will be the best day
of my entire life!*

*I get into the white Rolls Royce
a few hours later and soon
arrive at the chapel where the
wedding is being held, the
guests are already all there. I
wait behind the doors of the
chapel for Brittany to arrive.
When I eventually see the horse
and carriage pull up, I smile*

and the doors open and I walk down the aisle, this is the best moment of my life! As I hear the chapel doors open once more I try to resist the temptation to turn around, but I do, and when I see Brittany arm in arm with her dad walking down the aisle towards me, I feel like the luckiest man in the world!

Brittany

As I see Trevor turning his head
staring and smiling at me, my
heart melts like chocolate. My
bridesmaids keep their heads
forward as they walk in front
of me and as I get to the end I
hand Alex my white lily and
purple lavender Bouquet as all
of them stand next to Trevor's
groomsmen. Trevor takes my
hand, squeezing it tightly!
The vicar asks for everyone to
be seated then begins with, "We
are gathered here today to
witness the marriage of Trevor
Flanny-Tordjman and Brittany

Lynn Raymond. If anyone would like to object speak now or forever hold your peace,..... No? Good! Mr Raymond, do you accept Trevor to take your daughter in his hand of marriage?!"

"I certainly do!" says my dad. I feel relieved, and by the looks of it Trevor is too!

"Brittany, repeat after me,..... I, Brittany Lynn Raymond, take Trevor Flanny-Tordjman, to be my lawfully wedded husband."

I repeat the words then the vicar says "Trevor, do you accept Brittany's vows?"

"I do!" says Trevor, then Trevor says his vows and I say "I do!". Then we give each other the rings and the vicar pronounces us husband and wife! I'm Mrs.Tordjman!

Then we go to a pretty park and take some wedding photos and eventually arrive at the Next Step studio, also known as the filming studio, where the wedding party is happening! Bree is there and so is Frank. We have dinner then come the speeches. My dad does an embarrassing but sweet speech with pictures on a big screen,

then my mum, then Frank, then
my sister, then eventually
TREVOR!

Trevor

I begin my speech "Hello everyone, I'm just gonna get to the point. When I first met Brittany at the auditions for the Next Step, which is now shown worldwide, I just, it was love at first sight! She's my one and only and there was no way I knew that in just 3 and a half years time I would be married to her but I'm proud to call her my wife, Mrs.Tordjman. And I know she may be tricky to handle but I'm sure I can cope!" People laugh at this statement, especially her parents and our cast friends,

"Thank you to everyone who helped us through this happy and stressful time and especially Mr. Raymond who said yes to letting his daughter marry an odd guy like me but even more especially to Brittany, who said yes to me and is an amazing woman, who I want to spend the rest of my life with, thank you for making me the luckiest guy alive! Thank you!" I finish and see tears in my wife's beautiful eyes, I wipe them away, "That was beautiful, thank you" she says and we pull into a long kiss while everyone claps. Later it's time we give a present to the guests!

Brittany

After that touching speech earlier by MY HUSBAND, I am over the moon! We are going to do a dance for the guests, so I change into a purple, blue and white short mini dress, taking off my high heels, to be bare footed and Trevor wears a dark blue and white shirt and shorts with blue converse trainers. My bridesmaids change into white and black jumpsuits and they each have a groomsman to dance with. We dance to 'I need you now', with a sassy hip hop style and Trevor does a big

fancy lift with me and we end
in a kiss. The guests love it!

A few hours later at about 11pm
we leave to go on our
honeymoon which Trevor
planned! We get into the
carriage and wave to everyone,
like Royalty!
Eventually we arrive at the
airport and Trevor lets a pilot
lead me to a private plane and
I'm so shocked at how much
thought Trevor put into this,
this must have cost a fortune!
We watch films and kiss and
when I wake I'm on the brown
leather sofa leaning against

Trevor, my husband. Finally, after what feels like forever we land in someplace cold, Antartica! Trevor drives me through icy snow covered land on a snow mobile. We arrive at a large cabin with a boiling heated pool, this is Heaven! We have our first night together, as a married couple. It was an amazing night!

The next day....

Trevor and I slide into our steaming hot tub and kiss for a while, I'm wearing an orange and black bikini. I have been getting texts nonstop from my friends asking how it's going. There's so many I can't even read them all, never mind answer them all! Trevor has his strong arm around me in the hot tub! "How do you think I did?!" He asks "what, on the honeymoon, oh babe you did the best, it's so much fun!" I say! "Great!" He says pleased.

Trevor

A month and a week later....

We just got back from our honeymoon a week ago, Brittany and I are very happily married and fans are voting saying we're the cutest couple on the Next Step and in real life! Their calling us Jiley for the show and in real life Trittany! My wife, I believe, is the most beautiful woman on earth and the kindest! She's been going to charity autograph signings and interviews and concerts since we got back, I

was with her doing it too!
Brittany even met a girl in a
wheel chair with a serious
condition and invited her to
meet the whole cast at the
studio.
That night I brush my fingers
through Brittany's hair while
she sits next to me on the couch.
"Do you want children?!" asks
Brittany all of a sudden,
"Yeah, of course, in a few
years!" I answer contently,
"Me too!" She says agreeing,
"But in a few years!" she
quickly adds,
"Yeah, I agree." I answer happy
that she's not ready like me yet!

"We made it!" She said changing the conversation "even through when that Megan who played Beth actually in real life fancied you, you were loyal and stuck by my side and I love you for all of what you are, an actor, funny, kind, caring, loveable and handsome!" she says, and we share a loving smile at each other.

I had doubted getting married at the age of 20 but it was the best decision of my life and I'll never regret it! I lean in and we kiss for a long time as she holds onto my muscly neck and I hold onto her slim, smooth, soft, tanned waist, pulling her closer to me. When we finally pull apart, Brittany says "I start work at the 'Joanne Chapman School of Dance!' again next month." she said,

"Great, I'll be teaching at 'Raw Motion Dance' more now that we don't film 'The Next Step' again for another year and a half while they write the new script!" I tell her.

"That'll be nice, sharing your dance knowledge with children and teenagers less experienced!" Brittany encourages kindly, "Yeah, I'm really looking forward to it!" I answer enthusiastically. "Let's go to bed." I suggest, "Ok." She says in her natural Canadian voice.

Brittany

A year later....

I'm walking through to the living
room when I see a pile of post
at the door, fan mail. One letter
really stands out, it's a bright
shiny blue envelope with silver
glitter sprinkled on it and my
names written in a shiny purple
metallic pen. I gently pick it up
and dust of the cover, then tear
the envelope, Inside is a neatly
folded letter, I open it up and
read it:

Dear Brittany Raymond,

You are an amazing inspiration to so many girls out there! You probably hear that a million times every day but I just wanted to remind you to make it a million and one! I was so happy when I heard about your marriage to Trevor.

I know I'm a bit young (11) but LUCKY YOU! He is so handsome and kind and funny! I know you get lots of Fan-mail and probably won't read this but in case you do, I love you for what you are inside: a beautiful, kind, caring and an amazing person. You're also beautiful on the outside, might I add! And in case your ever in Scotland, come say 'Hi'! But I doubt that will happen because you're so busy in Canada doing what you love and spending time with Trevor. But

just in case there's a second of your
time come to.....
Love Emily Ruth Barker xxxx

I feel so loved as I read this! I
decide right then to write back,
and sign an autograph along
with it then put it in my mailbox
to be collected.
Then I decide, since it's nearly
Christmas, to bake.

Trevor

When I wake up from my nap I find Brittany baking and as she turns and smiles I walk up to her and put my arms around her waist as we kiss. Then I help her bake, although my side of the cooking tray for some reason didn't look as good as hers!

Brittany

A week later.....

Trevor eventually arrives home from Raw Motion Dance. I finished earlier than him at Joanne Chapman's so I am always home cooking dinner when he eventually comes home. There has been one thing on my mind for a while now and I think it's time to tell Trevor. When he gets home he kisses me on the cheek and sits down at the table as I do as well. "Trevor," I say nervously,

"Yeah babe" he says as he fills his plate with healthy things. "I've been thinking a lot and,... well, I want to have a child." I blurt out.

Trevor pauses for a second as he chews his salad and thinks, "Well, if your ready than I am too!" he says supportively!

"Really, I know we've only been married a year and a bit and I said it would be a few years but....."

Trevor cuts me off, "shhhhhhh, if this is what you want then I'm happy!" he says happily with a crack of nervousness.

So we decide to have a child as soon as we can!

A month later.....

It had been a month since that night and I had been feeling a bit uneasy since then, I was scared to take a test! I sat in the living room, I still had an hour till Trevor got back. I could go to the drugstore and take the test and hide it before Trevor got back, either hiding my disappointment or happiness! No, but I was so desperate to know. Oh, enough already, if I was pregnant I would have to take the test eventually anyway! So I get into Trevor's jet black Range Rover and drive to the store. I pause outside the door, knowing I was here now and had to do it! So I step inside the clean store and walk to the pregnancy section and nervously slide a box of 'clear blue' pregnancy tests of the shelf, I buy 2 then drive home fidgeting as I thought about the possibilities that 'stick' could show me. When I arrive home I change into a blue shirt that's Trevor's and take the test leaving it for 15 minutes afterwards to think about it.

When I hear the ping on my phone, I know the time is done so I walk through to the toilet and slowly turn over the blue and white test......positive plus 4 weeks, it says. "Ahhhhh" I scream excitedly, I take the other test and again it's positive! I'm so excited to be a mum. While I wait for Trevor to get home I am sitting on the kitchen cabinet checking on my phone about what pregnancy feels like, I find one website that is NOT helpful at all, it says morning sickness is awful and the entire thing is sore and that you'll look fat and ugly.

I posted an angry comment on there saying that 'they should explain the good things and explain nicely how to get through the bad things.'

I add lots of extra angry bits In between. Soon I hear the roar of Trevor's other car and the screeching of gravel under the wheels. When I hear the click of the door key in the knob, I run to the door and hug his sweaty body, obviously tired out from dancing at 'Raw Motion Dance'. "Hey babe" he says exhausted as he drops his sports bag. "Can I speak with you for a moment?!" I ask nervously,

"Course!" He says a little more energetically. So we get some butter n' honey popcorn and hot berry juice and snuggle up in bed and switch on TV. Then is the right moment to tell him, when he's relaxed, so I stroke his black hair and he turns to look into my chocolatey brown eyes, I kiss him then tell him the news, "Babe?" I ask

"Yeah?!" He says looking at me. "Well, we started trying to have a baby a month ago and well today I.....1 minute!" I get out of bed and walk into the bathroom to retrieve the test from the draw under the tap. I get it then walk back through, "I think you might want to see this.." I say scared at what his reaction might be as I hand him it.

Trevor

I take whatever Brittany
handed me, still looking up at
her, with a crease of concern on
my forehead and a look of
worry in my eyes. As I finally
look down at the long piece of
heavy plastic I'm holding I see
the words 'positive plus 4
weeks' "whaaaa.....?????" I ask
confused, then I realise, "OH
MY WORD! YOUR
PREGNANT!" I shout, I watch
as she nods at me nervously, I
look up at my wife's pretty face
and smile, then I'm jumping off
the bed and holding her in my

arms. "This is amazing, we're going to be parents!" I say to her as she hugs me, lifting her feet of the floor in excitement. "Really, you're pleased?!" She asks seeming surprised. "Yes! I agreed to this!" I say reassuringly. We kiss and we have the most happy of nights, watching TV and ordering stuff for the new arrival!

Brittany

11 weeks later.....

I'm 15 weeks pregnant now and we've told our parents and the cast, who are all overjoyed and are postponing the filming of season 5 till the babies 6 months old. Our first exam at the hospital took ages! As I look in the mirror that day, I notice a small bump poking out and I lift up my top and feel it, Trevor comes through and hugs me and the bump and asks "what's wrong babe?"

I answer "I'm getting FAT!".
Trevor only laughs at this, "IT'S
NOT FUNNY!" I insist.
"I know, but your still just as
beautiful to me!" he says
lovingly.
"I love you!" I say,
" I love you just as much but
times a billion!" He says!
Today is my 4th doctors exam
and I'm meant to be getting a
new doctor. When I get there I
sign in and wait sitting on
Trevor's strong knee. Eventually
Trevor and I are called in so we
join hands and walk into the
plain room. I lie on the bed and
eventually the doctor comes in,

MEGAN, so this is what she meant when she said she had a new career path in mind and left acting! I thought we were done with her.

"BRITTANY AND NO?....TREVOR!" she screeches, she surprisingly looks quite smart and doctorish.

"Umm, YO!" Trevor blurts out. I'm just stunned, SHE'S delivering OUR baby! Not on my watch! "Megan, hi nice to see you again but I'm not sure this will work, Trevor and I are MARRIED!" I say, with a little more temper than I meant.

"Chill, I'm engaged to the man

of my dreams, I'm sorry to you both for what I did, trying to break you up but I've moved on and I've heard all about you and Trevor the marriage and the love! So I hope you can forgive me!" she says kindly and innocently and I believe her, maybe she is a changed woman! I look up at Trevor and he nods then leans down and kisses me, "thank you, I'm sorry too and congrats on the engagement!" I say sweetly,

"Thank you, good!" she says happily! Then the exam begins and she smears the clear cold jelly on my stomach and wiggles

the ultrasound wand around
and I see my dark fuzzy baby
on the ultrasound TV. I look up
at Trevor and he's smiling too!
"Everything looks good there!"
Megan says and then takes the
baby's heartbeat, followed by
taking my blood pressure and
my pulse! Once it's over Trevor
and I go to a cafe and order
some hot cocoa as its March
and its just started snowing!
When we get home I climb onto
the sofa with a TNS duvet over
me and I drink hot soup and
Trevor tickles and kisses the
little bump on my tummy, then I
get up and begin preparing

dinner because Vic is coming
for dinner tonight with Alex so I
need to be ready for when they
arrive.

I thought about how lucky I
have been with my morning
sickness, only having it mildly!
When they arrive they squeal
and peek down at my blooming
tummy! We have a salad dinner,
as dancers we don't want to be
FAT, unfortunately I'm pregnant
so I can't help it! Trevor Kisses
my head then heads out to have
a boys night at Isaacs, watching
football and talking about all
the weird things happening to
me during my pregnancy! Gross

and Embarrassing! Vic and Alex ask how we're going to tell the fans, as we haven't told them yet! "Well, we're going wait till I'm about 16 weeks, in 1 weeks time, then we'll get Trevor's mums dog to walk in to next weeks concert holding a sign saying 'Brittany and Trevor are pregnant!' He's a really well trained dog!" I tell their interested faces, "awwwww, that's so sweet!" They say in unison. After dinner we have a low fat coffee and we talk about the night of my wedding a year and a few months ago!

Then I hug them both and they leave. About an hour later Trevor gets home........

Trevor

....As I walk through the front door Brittany flings her arms around my body and I dump my bag then give her a big kiss. When we pull apart Brittany asks "How was Isaac's?" "Good, Canada won the game!" I tell her, "That's great, honey!" she says, then we're so tired we go to bed.

The next day......

I wake up cuddling my wife and slip out of bed, now Brittany's pregnant she's been really hot, lazy and hungry for odd and specific things! So I leave her to sleep and go down stairs. Just 5 more days till she's 4 months pregnant! I make some pancakes and as I'm flipping one, Britts comes downstairs, I grin at her and leave the pancakes for a minute to kiss her, then she offers to continue the pancake while I get ready..... When I'm ready I go back downstairs to find Brittany panicking as she's set the stove on fire, she's blowing and using a tea towel to fan it! I rush over and grab the drink of water I had, then I pour it over

the fire and it extinguishes!
"Brittany, what are you doing?
You could of set the whole
house on fire!" I warn angrily,
"Sorry babe, I was trying to
make the pancakes cook quicker
while I tossed them!" She
apologises,
"It's ok, it's just pregnancy
hormones acting up and giving
you weird ideas." I say
soothingly, hugging her to me
closely and protectively and
kiss her forehead. Well that's
another job, fixing the stove!
So I called the handyman and
he's coming tomorrow to fix it

while we're at Brittany's extra pregnancy exam.

Brittany

The next day........

I wake up the next day and Trevor is already ready. "come on, sweetheart! We'll be late for the exam!" he says,
"Sorry," I say and set to brushing my hair and teeth, then I pull on a plain white long sleeved top and scruffy jeans, then I pull on a navy blue scarf with grey specks on it and black ankle boots. Then I put some peach lipstick on, eyeliner, concealer and mascara. I am ready within 20 minutes. As I

walk out the door while Trevor holds it open he strokes my short smoky brownish blonde hair and kisses my head. Then we climb into the car and Trevor starts the engine.

"Hopefully Megan will be as off me as she was last week!" says Trevor trying to make a joke! I laugh and kiss his shoulder. Then I cup my womb, "Hey little person, I'm your mummy, I'm very excited to meet you, I'll give you lots of hugs and kisses when you do arrive!" I say, looking down at my tummy, talking to the baby inside me. Trevor side glances at me and smiles as he drives. When I get to the hospital and Trevor pulls the brake and locks the car once we've gotten out. We walk inside hand in hand, I sign in and then sit in the waiting area holding Trevor's hand as we sit and I nervously tap my foot. "You nervous?" Asks Trevor, "Yeah, I've been here a few times now but I can't help feeling a little nervous for the baby's safety." I answer, "I know," he says and tightly squeezes my hand. He kisses me and we stay like that for a while then pull apart. We sit there for another 5 minutes and then a little girl with crutches hobbles up, "ARE YOU BRITTANY AND TREVOR TORDJMAN?!" shrieks the little girl,

"Yes we are!" I tell her,

"Oh my word, I love the next step and Jiley and Trittany! Can I have your autograph?!" she asks,

"Of course!" Trevor says, so she hands me her little notebook and pen and me and Trevor sign it!

"Thank you!" she says then she hugs us and her mum smiles as a thanks and pulls her away.

"That was close!" I say to

Trevor, "I was scared she might ask why we're in the hospital's maternity department!" I tell him,

"Yeah! Phew!" Says Trevor. Finally we're called in and the exam goes well, Megan is nice and the baby and I are well. Afterwards Trevor and I go for a walk, occasionally stopping to sign autographs and take pictures.

5 days later.....

Today is the day of the concert where we'll tell all the fans about my pregnancy. I am dressed in a red maternity mini dress made of soft material and lace. I have my hair styled as best as it can be due to the length and I'm wearing red high heels. I have a black cashmere duffel to hide my bump as well and red lipstick, black eyeshadow, concealer, eyeliner and mascara as well as perfect eyebrows as always! Trevor's wearing a tux with a bow tie. We get into the White limo and arrive at the concert with Trevor's mums dog and we put the sign in his teeth and he walks down the red carpet like a professional, enjoying the attention. People hush as they see the sign, then as we step out there's a huge cheer of people shouting 'cute way to tell us' and 'awwwwwww' and 'congrats!' We smile and take pictures and sign autographs, then we get inside and walk up to the stage as all our friends prepare backstage.

"HELLO CANADA!" Trevor yells,

"Now you might not have seen the sign Trevor's mums dog carried in but just to tell you I will not be dancing tonight, Trevor will though, because........We're expecting!" I yell into the microphone, I hear a large cheer and smile, then we walk of the stage and Trevor and I go backstage. I sit in the wings and watch as Trevor and all my friends dance amazingly!

Trevor

The next day......

When I wake up the next day, I'm shocked to find Brittany out of bed before me. Brittany's wearing a floaty short purple top, black leggings, black shoes, a silver love heart necklace and purple and black sunglasses as well as dark pink lip-gloss and her usual make up. She's eating a pickle sandwich in the kitchen and some coke mixed with fanta! Those are some odd pregnancy cravings! I kiss her head and she offers me a pickle

sandwich but I quickly say no!
"What are we going to do
today?" I ask, suddenly,
Brittany stops eating and holds
a hand to her stomach and
moans. "What's wrong baby?!" I
ask alarmed,
"owwwwww!" she screeches,
"what's going on?!" She asks.
So we get in the car and drive
to hospital. I wait worriedly
and impatiently in the waiting
room.
Eventually Brittany comes
out..... I jump up and run to her
and touch her shoulder, "what
happened?!" I ask, "sorry Hun,
false alarm, the babies first

kick, it's growing Hun, I can feel it!" She tells me excitedly. So as not to waste our time out we go to a cafe.

"Honey, we can't keep calling the baby 'it' it just makes me feel bad, I love this baby and I want to know its name when it comes into the world!" she says,

"Uh huh, well maybe we should find out the gender!" I say,

"Yeah, that's a good idea, but names!" She asks, "I really want to name it Riley if it's a girl after my role on The Next Step and how about James for a boy?!" she asks,

"Yeah! I love that idea!" I tell her honestly,

"Great! I'll schedule an appointment to find out the sex!" she says pleased. So as soon as she says that, she's on her phone arranging it! She schedules it for the next day.

The next day......

Today is the day we find out the sex of the baby and Brittany is overreacting with excitement!

Brittany

I kiss Trevor good morning and make myself a low fat coffee and drink it. I wash in the bath and tie my hair up in a short pony tail, after brushing it. Then I brush my teeth and put on my makeup, eyeliner, red lipstick, mascara and concealer as well as the eyebrow pencil. Then I pull on a dark red long sleeved top with beige buttons opened at the neck, blue jeans and white trainers. Trevor is in a short sleeved grey T-shirt and black shorts with black converse. "Trevor! Come on!

We'll be late!" I tell him crossly as he puts gel in his hair to give him his cute little black quiff! "Ok, ok! I'm coming!" he says. When he's done I pull him by the arm out to the car and he climbs in, purposely taking ages to do his seatbelt, waiting for my reaction. "TREVOR!" I yell, "Ok, sorry!" He says clearly caught out! Then we drive to the maternity department in the hospital. When I arrive I rush in and sign in and I end up having to wait anxiously for 10 whole minutes. I'm acting like an impatient 5 year old I realise and sit back relaxing,......a bit.

Trevor knows I'm nervous and takes my hand squeezing it tightly the way he does and I say "I love you!" and he says "I love you just as much times a billion!" I kiss him passionately and we lean our foreheads against each other. Then Megan calls us in and I anxiously sit on the bed seat. "How we doing?!" She asks,

"Good!" Trevor answers for me. Then the examination begins. Once again she squirts the cold clear jelly onto my stomach and moves about the wand, Trevor holds my hand the whole time. "I can't be sure but through the

ultrasound it looks like your
having a.........GIRL!" Says
Megan,
"Riley!" I breath quietly and
love is born. Trevor smiles down
at me and said,
"a girl, our little Riley!"
"Now as I said we can't be sure
but I'm pretty positive it is!"
says Megan, but as she tells me
this it feels like a girl! Then we
go to get my professional
pregnancy photos, which come
out beautifully!

5 months later.....

I'm lying in bed on the 21st of August when my water breaks and I get an awful pain. "Trevor, Trevor, TREVOR!" I shout-whisper, as I shake him awake, finally he wakes up, "wha...what....!!!!! What's happening?!" he says panicking, I roll my eyes, I love Trevor and all, but BOYS, HONESTLY! "I'm in labour!" I tell him in a panicky voice, "oh no! Ok stay calm! I'll get the bags and start the engine, you lie down!" Trevor says kindly and jumps up from the bed. I love him! Finally he bundles me in the car and holds my hand

with one hand. When we arrive
he signs in and fills in some
sheets of paper and then we get
into a birthing room. I lie in the
bed and eventually Megan
comes through, she smiles at me
kindly and holds my hand,
"You're doing great! Keep
doing what your doing, Trevor's
just getting a low fat coffee to
keep him awake, as its 2am!"
says Megan, and as she turns to
exit, I call her, and she walks
over,
"Thankyou!" I tell her weakly.
Trevor eventually comes in and
helps me through each
contraction, checking the heart

rate for me and Riley. Hours go
by...............
And at 6am Riley's born! She
cries hysterically as she comes
into the world,
"congratulations!" says Megan
and gets the midwife to get a
blanket for her but nothing can
break this moment: just me,
Trevor and now, Riley! I cradle
her as Trevor stands and
strokes Riley and my hair. I
wrap her in the pink blanket the
midwife gave me and snuggle
her close to me, she has jet
black tufty hair and glistening
blue eyes unlike Trevor and I
who have brown eyes. She has a

light pink little lips. She's
beautiful!

Trevor

I stand next to my wife as we both stare down at our new daughter, Riley! I lean down as my wife looks up and kiss her. "She looks like you!" I say to Brittany as Riley plays with Brittany's big finger, "I think she has your ears and lips, though!" Brittany says as Riley falls into an adorable sleep. I look down at my perfect wife and new daughter, I'm the luckiest guy alive! Eventually Riley wakes up and the midwife gives her her first bath as I stand watching, meanwhile

Brittany has fallen into a happy sleep. After Riley's bath the midwife lets me change her into the outfit Brittany chose for her, it's a light yellow and grey dress with delicate little pop out thin white fake flowers spread about it, a matching headband and a matching cloth diaper. Then I pick her up and cuddle her to me. I'm a dad! When Brittany wakes up she smiles weakly and says 3 simple words "I'm a mommy!" We tell each other we love each other as we stare down at our beloved daughter! Life is perfect!

5 months later......

Our beautiful daughter is 5
months old but still tiny and
always beautiful. Riley has her
ears pierced too. We'll be
filming season 5 of the next
step next month! I Take a
picture of Brittany and Riley as
they sleep in our King sized
bed.
The whole cast loves her and
the fans! Riley's wearing a
white fluffy polar bear sleeper
with small round ears poking
out of it at the hood. Brittany
cuddles her and kisses her
head.

Brittany

1 year later.......

Riley has grown fast and her hair has changed a dark brown colour instead of jet black like when she was born, more like me than Trevor now, it's short and straight, which is above her neck, very short. She can't quite walk but she can crawl, she needs help when she walks if she does. She's big baby size. She loves watching the Next Step and her favourite characters are her daddy and I,

Riley and James — she has not worked out they are us yet! She is enrolled in dance classes and is currently doing ballet. She's beautiful as always! And yes life is perfect, we're filming the last season (Season 8) of 'The Next Step!' In June, 2 months away! ....

We are currently at a TNS cast and crew barbecue.

"Sweetie! No!" I say as Riley grabs for a lock of Vic's beautiful blonde hair, Vic laughs,

"It's ok! She's grown so fast!" she says,

"I know! She's still figuring out her first word though!",
"You're so lucky you've built a whole family, a husband, a daughter! I'm still trying to find the right man! I mean, Alex fell in love and is engaged and so did Jennie, who's expecting her first kid!",
I feel a pang of sympathy for Vic as she says this, "Well, I know someone who likes you!" I tell her honestly,
"Who?!" She asks surprised,
"That guy friend of yours, I don't know his name!" I tell her,
"noooooo, Brandon, really?!",
"Yes!" I say, "well maybe I'll

talk to him the next time I see him!" she says, suddenly excited. Jennie walks over holding her husbands hand, a guy from a whirlwind holiday romance, they got married a month after they met! The baby is coming in 1 month and they got married 1 year ago. Victoria kisses Riley's cheek and walks over to talk to Taveeta, Lamar, Isaac and Alex. Trevor walks over and starts talking to Charlie, Jennies husband. "I can't believe how amazing it feels to have a life growing inside of you!" she tells me,

"I know, but just wait till they come into the world. Riley's MY miracle and so is Trevor." I tell her as Riley drifts of to sleep on my knee, "Jennie strokes her stomach happily.

"Do you know whether it'll be a boy or a girl yet?!" I ask,

"Maybe, ok yes we do but we don't want to tell any.....oh, alright, a boy, a beautiful bouncing baby boy!" She tells me happily, "That's wonderful! Congratulations!" I say,

"We're naming him Tristan!" she tells me,

"Lovely!" I say, as I smooth out Riley's designer baby clothes—a

small light pink dress with a
flower patterns on the top part.

Trevor

1 month later......

I hug my wife and small 1 year
and 6 month old daughter, we
just heard the news that
Victoria and her boy friend,
Brandon, have just become
more than friends (boyfriend
and girlfriend), like my wife
had suggested to her! Victoria
said she thinks he might be the
one! Life is perfect and Jennie
had her baby 3 days ago and he
is adorable, I'm the same old me,
funny at most and Brittany
wants another child in 2 years

when Riley's 3! I'll admit that took a little bit of persuasion towards me! But hey! We're a family and we couldn't be more happy! So.....bye!

The End!

Dedicated to Brittany Raymond, Trevor Tordjman, The Next Step cast, Butternut my dog and my family.

Made in the USA
Charleston, SC
03 November 2015